Will *and* Wisdom

what *about* Christmas?

Art Direction and Design: David Riley Associates, Newport Beach, California Rileydra.com

Published in 2016 by Will and Wisdom Books, Newport Beach, California
and BluSky Publishers, Franklin, Tennessee

ISBN 978-0-9846349-9-6

This book belongs to

....

Will and *Wisdom* were at the mall

two days before Christmas doing some

last minute shopping. They listened as

a little boy talked with Santa.

"I want a new bike and I want

some video games and a lot of

money and a bunch of other stuff

too." Suddenly, the boy noticed

Wisdom looking at him.

"What do you want, giant hamster?"

the little boy asked. "Actually, I am

a guinea pig," said *Wisdom*. "And I

don't want anything, but I am amazed

at how much you want."

"Well, it's Christmas," the little

boy informed *Wisdom*. "Christmas

is all about presents."

Will smiled because he knew what

Wisdom was going to say next. "So,

you think that Christmas is all about

presents?" questioned *Wisdom*. "Isn't

it?" asked the little boy.

Wisdom then asked the little boy

if he would like to hear the story of

the very first Christmas. The little boy

nodded his head 'yes' and *Wisdom*

began to tell the story.

"Around two thousand years ago a

young pregnant woman named Mary

and her husband Joseph traveled for

many days to a city called Bethlehem.

The city was filled with people who

had come from far away so all of the

rooms at the inn were taken. Thankfully,

the innkeeper let Mary and Joseph

sleep in his barn.

Then one night Mary gave birth to

a baby boy. She wrapped him in strips of

cloth and laid him in a manger. There were

shepherds out in the field near the city

watching sheep that night.

O

Suddenly, the angel of the Lord appeared to

them and said, 'Fear not, for I am bringing you good

news of great joy for all people. Today, in the city

of Bethlehem a Savior has been born. He is Christ

the Lord. You will find the baby wrapped in cloths

sleeping in a manger.'"

When *Wisdom* finished the story

he smiled and said, "That is the story of the

first Christmas and how God sent His Son

Jesus into the world." The little boy smiled

and gave *Wisdom* a hug.

THE END

For unto you is born this day in the city of David a Savior, which is Christ the Lord.

Luke 2:11

A Prayer To Follow God
and Become a Christian

Dear God,

Help me to be giving and do the right things.
I believe you love me so much that you gave your
only Son, Jesus, to die on the cross for the things
that I have done wrong. Please forgive me and
come into my life and change me. I believe that
Jesus rose from the dead and is coming back some
day. Until then, I will follow you for the rest of my
life. Jesus is my God, my Savior and my forever
Friend. In Jesus' Name, Amen.

_____   _____

your name   date

If you have just prayed that prayer and meant it with all your heart, you are a child of God and will live with Him forever in heaven.

Here's what you can do now:

1. Read the Bible to learn more about God.

2. Go to church and worship with other believers.

3. Be baptized so that others know of your commitment to follow God.

4. Pray everyday and thank the Lord for all that you have.

5. Know that you can do and accomplish anything with God in your life.